Christopher Radko
Memories of Yesteryear

Andrews McMeel
Publishing®

Kansas City

02 03 04 05 06 LEO 10 9 8 7 6 5 4 3 2 1
ISBN: 0-7407-2511-4
Library of Congress Catalog Card Number: 2001099431

Edited by Charlie Colborne
Designed by Eric Schotland

Attention: Schools and Businesses
Andrews McMeel books are available at quantity discounts with bulk purpose for education, business, or sales promotional use. For information please write to: Special Sales Department, Andrews McMeel Publishing, 4520 Main Street, Kansas City, Missouri 64111.

Christopher Radko

Memories of Yesteryear

Christmas
IS NO TIME FOR RESTRAINT!

— Christopher Radko

My Favorite

THIS one is my favorite —
or maybe that one, there.
This one's really ancient —
that one's REALLY RARE.
Here's one I grew up with . . .
this one is brand new . . .
Which one is my favorite?
I can't pick — can you?

Wheaton Malahy

In the Attic

We find them in the attic,
those boxes filled with cheer—
Dust them of their cobwebs
'cause Christmastime is here.

Now for decorations!
The bulbs, the lights, the trees!
Garlands full of glitter . . .
and Christmas memories.

The Santa mugs and saucers,
the stockings stitched with love,
the statue of the snowman,
the precious crystal dove.

All these festive trimmings
Play a special part
in keeping Christmas memories
Shining in the heart!

Charlie Colborne

Winter Weather Advisory

FROST *is on the windows*

And snowflakes soon will start—

To WARM YOURSELF *this winter,*

Keep Christmas in your heart!

Dan Byrne

12

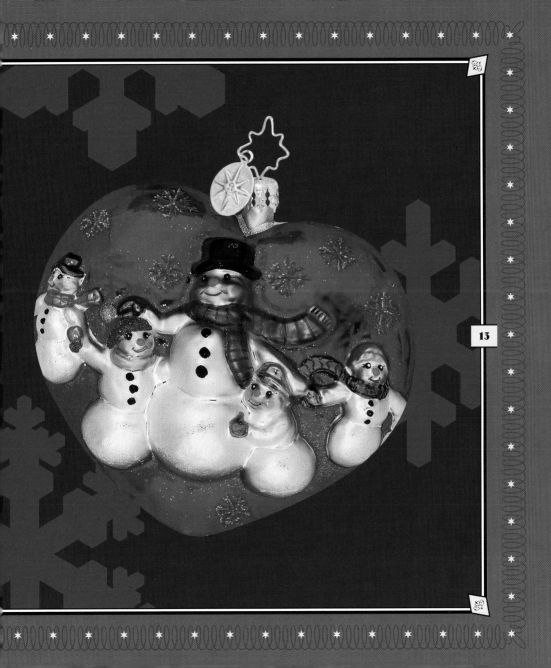

We're Caroling This Evening

We're CAROLING this evening —
I hope you brought your coat!
We'll sing a song of Christmas
With joy in every note!

⸺⸺⸺

We haven't had much practice —
We know these songs by HEART.
There might be too much eggnog,
So I hope you KNOW YOUR PART!

Charlie Colborne

A Christmas to Remember

The candles are lit,
The CRANBERRIES chilled,
The turkey is carved,
The gravy boat's filled.

Delicious aromas,
HOLIDAY CHEER . . .
A Christmastime FEAST
To remember all year.

Carroll Lincoln

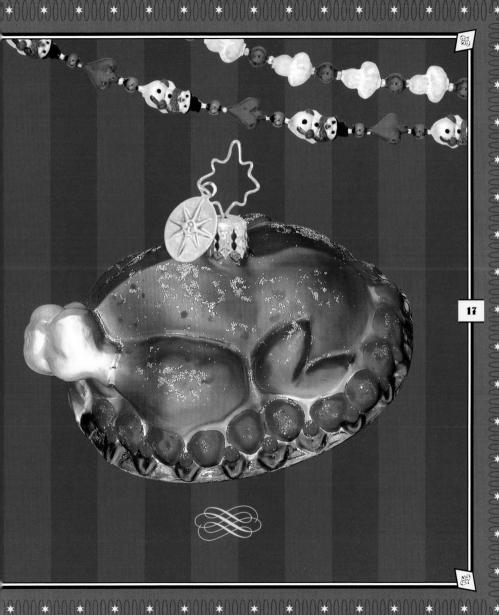

As a kid, I knew Christmas

was **FINALLY** really here

when Mom got out

the CHRISTMAS ORNAMENTS.

That was excitement!

Dan Byrne

Putting Up the Tree

We're putting up the tree TONIGHT!
We're putting up the tree!
We picked it out ourselves and it's
as tall as tall can be!

✦ ✦ ✦

IT TOWERS past the ceiling —
It stretches to the sky,
And airplanes fly around it
When they are passing by!

✦ ✦ ✦

It reaches up to heaven,
And when it goes that far,
It bumps into the MILKY WAY
And gets the brightest star!

Jan Miller Girando

Nutcracker Parade

1 — 2 — 3 — 4
Nutcrackers MARCHING
in your door.

3 — 1 — 4 — 2
Nutcrackers marching
past your SHOE.

4 — 2 — 1 — 3
Nutcrackers marching
UP your tree.

2 — 4 — 3 — 1
Nutcrackers marching —
now they're done!

Jan Miller Girando

The Tree and Dove

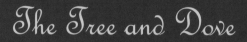

Christmastime —
    the tree and dove,
All traditions
    that we love.
We're pieces of
    a greater thing.
Listen —
    the angels sing:
      comfort & joy!
      comfort & joy!

Charlie Colborne

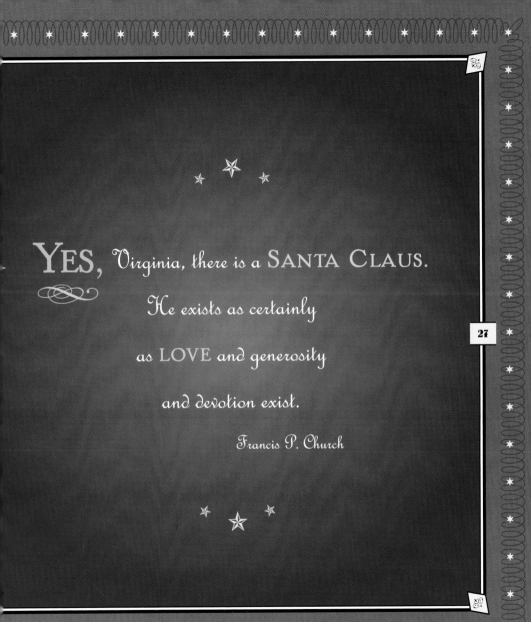

YES, Virginia, there is a SANTA CLAUS.

He exists as certainly

as LOVE and generosity

and devotion exist.

Francis P. Church

Home-Baked Gifts

✳ ✳ ✳ ✳ ✳ ✳ ✳ ✳ ✳

A chocolate cake

WHIPPED up from scratch,

Christmas cookies

By the BATCH,

A pumpkin pie,

A lemon tart . . .

Home-baked gifts

To warm the HEART!

Wheaton Malahy

Little Teeny Tree

I have a teeny Christmas tree
that's trimmed with TEENY lights
And little teeny ornaments
that hang from teeny HEIGHTS!

A little teeny garland
is SWAGGED from sprig to sprig.
My Christmas tree is teeny —
the joy it brings is BIG.

Jan Miller Girando

Brrrr!
It's never too COLD for a snowman!
A blizzard is what he likes best!
He puts on his scarf and he's ready
to pass any wintery test!

His little coal eyes twinkle brightly.
He twitches his nose with such glee —
It's never too cold for a snowman,
but it might be too cold for ME!

Carroll Lincoln

Two Friends

♦ ♦ ♦

Very MERRY—
that, we were!
I HAD WRAPPED
a gift for her.
She had, unexpectedly,
packaged up
a gift for ME!
Customs old, yet ever new . . .
Very merry FRIENDS,
we two!

Jan Miller Girando

The HEART of Christmas

is warmth and GOODWILL to others.

Dan Byrne

"God bless US every one!"

Charles Dickens
A Christmas Carol

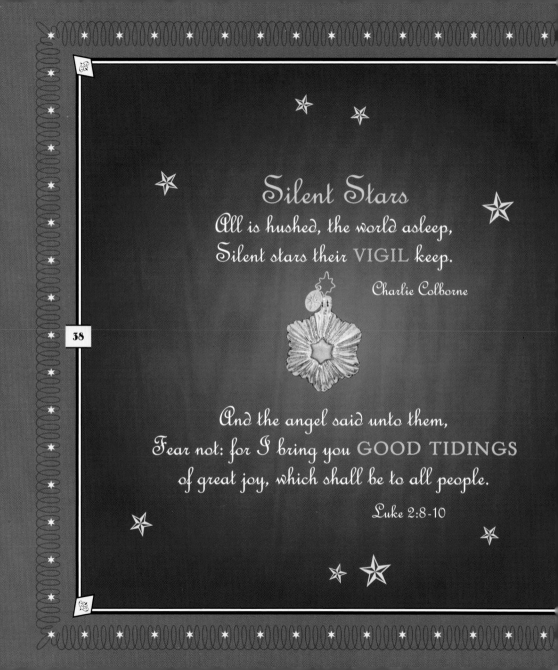

Silent Stars

All is hushed, the world asleep,
Silent stars their VIGIL keep.

Charlie Colborne

And the angel said unto them,
Fear not: for I bring you GOOD TIDINGS
of great joy, which shall be to all people.

Luke 2:8-10

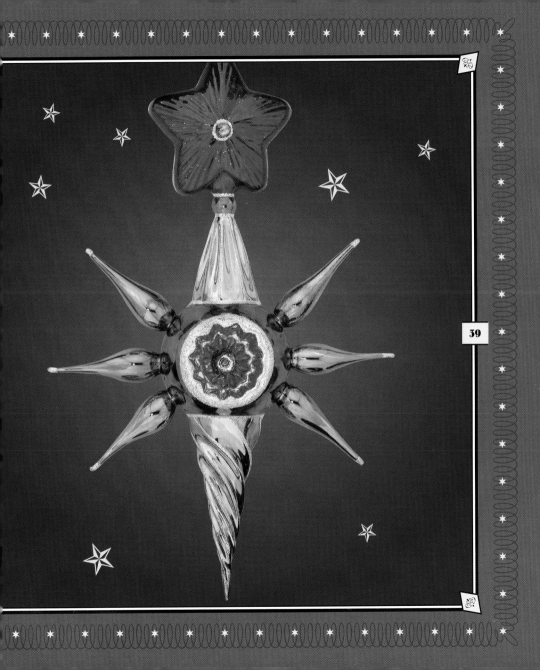

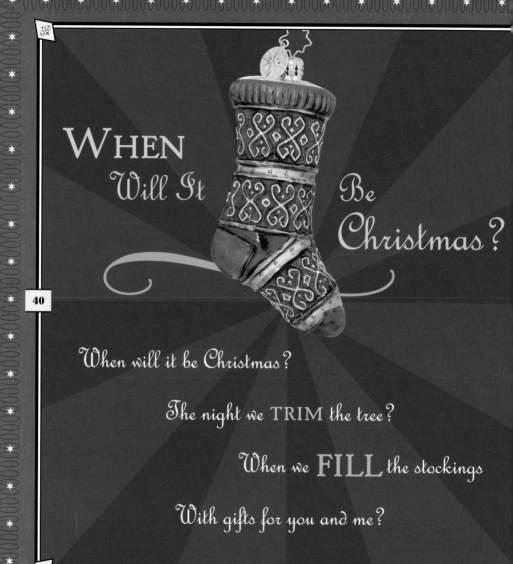

WHEN
Will It
Be
Christmas?

When will it be Christmas?

The night we TRIM the tree?

When we FILL the stockings

With gifts for you and me?

WAIT! I just remembered,

There's no official start —

Christmas is whenever

You FEEL it in your heart.

Kay Hegarty

My Companion

My kitty knows it's Christmastime . . .
she **PURRS** a winter purr.
I give her Christmas catnip toys
and brush her silky fur.
I play with her and **TOSS** her favorite
toys around the room.
With elegance, she sits unmoved.
So tell me — who owns whom?

Carroll Lincoln

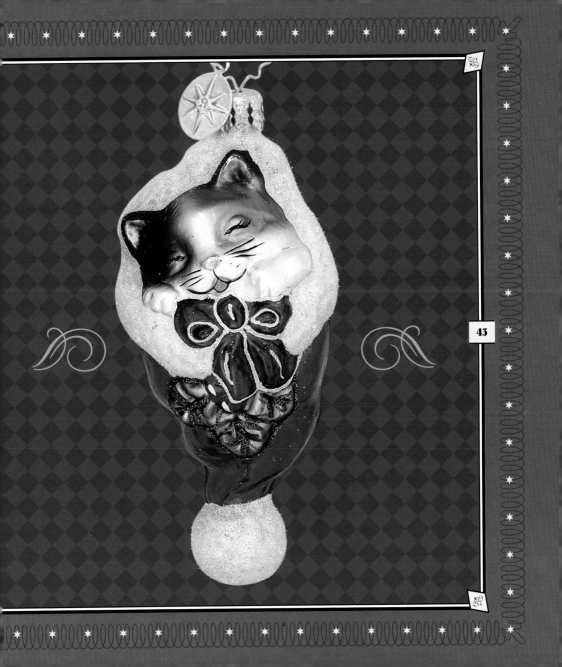

Christmas Is Coming!

Christmas is coming,
the GEESE are getting fat,

Please to put a penny in
the old man's hat;

If you haven't got a penny,
a ha' penny will do,

IF you haven't got a ha' penny,
God bless you.

Old English Carol

Finery

"I am reticent," she said,
"to put that hat upon my head.
Christmastime or not, I know
feathers simply DO NOT GO."

Jan Miller Girando

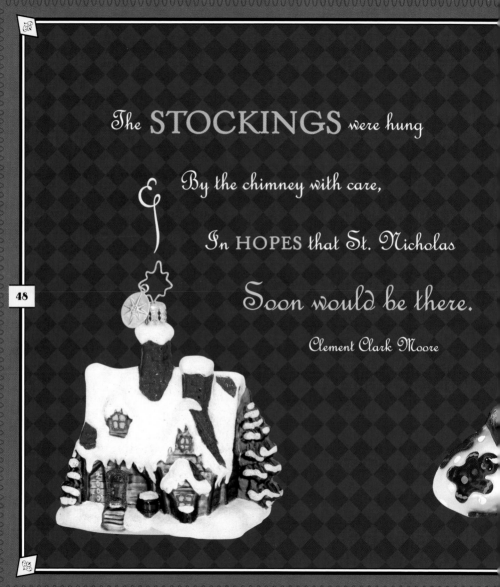

The STOCKINGS were hung

By the chimney with care,

In HOPES that St. Nicholas

Soon would be there.

Clement Clark Moore

◎ The Orange ◎

There's an orange in the toe of the STOCKING
That I hung from the mantle with care.
There's a TREAT that is mine for the taking —
I can see from the shape that it's there.

⌒

Guess that Santa forgot I'd been crabby —
Or maybe his elves didn't see
The times I talked back to my mother
And FLOUNCED about bad as can be.

⌒

There's an orange in the toe of my stocking,
And I HOPE it's not making a hole...
If I reach down inside, I can feel it...
I'VE GOT IT!

But OH NO. . .

it's COAL!!

Jan Miller Girando

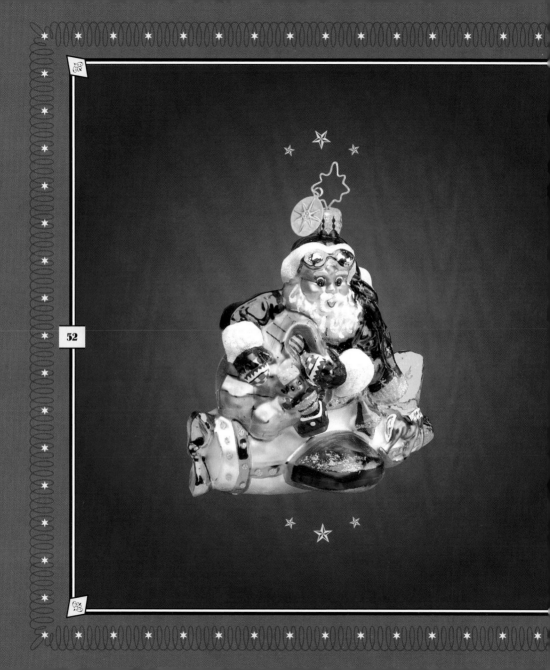

52

Special Delivery

·~~~~~~·

IT WOULDN'T BE CHRISTMAS
WITHOUT OLD ST. NICK.

HE'S SIMPLY ESSENTIAL —
HE MAKES IT ALL TICK!

HE'S JOLLY (AND CHUBBY)
AND FILLED WITH DELIGHT.

HE FLIES THROUGH THE AIR
ON ONE GLORIOUS NIGHT.

~

THE JOY THAT HE'S BRINGING
IS LEGEND INDEED. . .

HOW DOES HE DO IT?
WHAT MAGIC! WHAT
SPEED!

AS CHRISTMAS APPROACHES,
HE PACKS UP HIS SLEIGH.

HE STUDIES HIS LIST
AND HE'S OFF ON HIS WAY!

ALL OVER THE WORLD,
NOT A CHILD GOES TO SLEEP —

THEY'RE PEERING FROM WINDOWS
TO CATCH JUST A PEEP
OF REINDEER AND SLEIGH BELLS
AND ZILLIONS OF TOYS
THAT SANTA IS BRINGING
TO GOOD GIRLS AND BOYS.

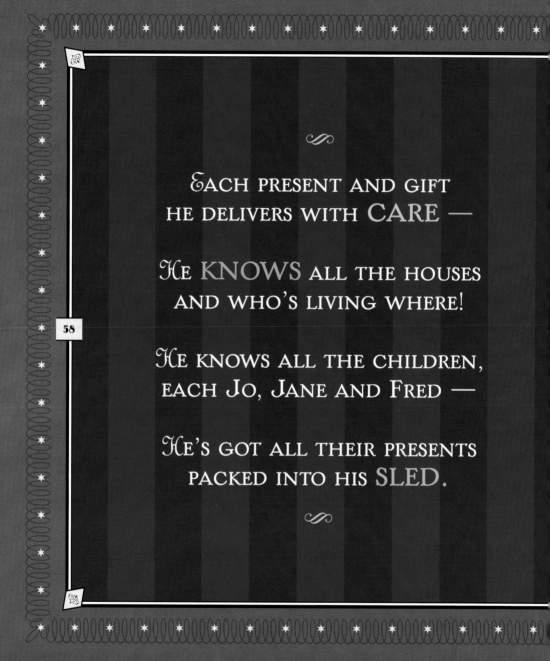

Each present and gift
he delivers with CARE —

He KNOWS all the houses
and who's living where!

He knows all the children,
each Jo, Jane and Fred —

He's got all their presents
packed into his SLED.

AND WHEN THEY'RE DELIVERED,
HE NODS TO HIS TEAM —

THEY'RE OFF IN A FLASH
LIKE A WINTERY DREAM.

AND EACH HAPPY CHILD
WILL AWAKE TO THE SIGHT

OF THE MAGIC THAT HAPPENED
THAT ONE CHRISTMAS NIGHT.

Charlie Colborne

AS EVENING FELL and shadows

stretched across the carpet, the glowing

Christmas lights created a jeweled pool

in the room. The tree was complete.

One by one, they had CAREFULLY hung

each precious ornament. . . but they

had trimmed the TREE in memories.

Wheaton Malahy

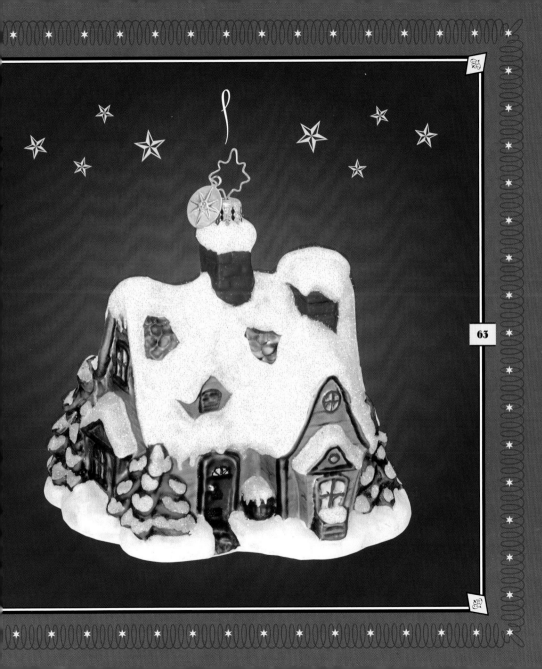

Second Helpings

One potato, ◆ ◆ ◆

TWO potatoes,

Three potatoes,

Four. . .

Mashed potatoes,

Sweet potatoes. . .

Serve me up S'MORE!

Jan Miller Girando

Grandpa's Rumble Seat

We're **DASHING** through the woods,
Our spirits oh so bright!
We're packed in Grandpa's rumble seat —
We really are a SIGHT!

We're tooting on the HORN,
Though nothing's in our way —
The trusty roadster helps *ring in*
Our favorite holiday!

Dan Byrne

Be of good CHEER.

William Shakespeare

I heard the BELLS on Christmas Day
Their old, familiar carols play,
And wild and sweet
Their words repeat
Of PEACE on earth, good will to men!

Henry Wadsworth Longfellow

A glad HEART makes a cheerful countenance.

Proverbs 15:13

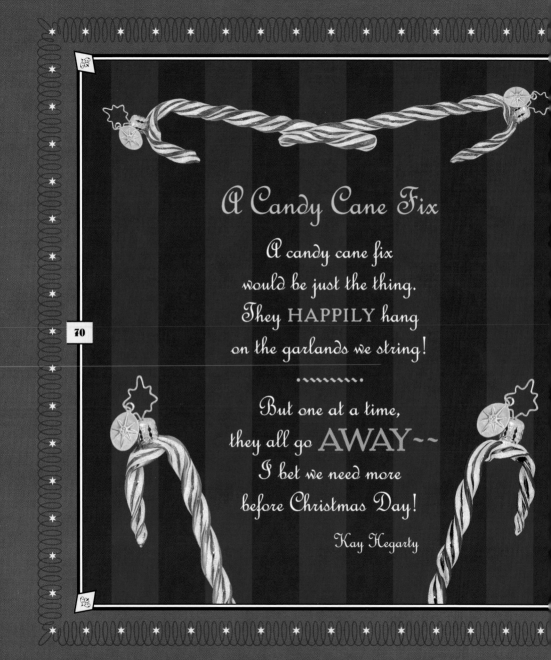

A Candy Cane Fix

A candy cane fix
would be just the thing.
They HAPPILY hang
on the garlands we string!

·~~~~~~~~·

But one at a time,
they all go AWAY~~
I bet we need more
before Christmas Day!

Kay Hegarty

A Winter Walk

A **WALK** in the winter...

snow crunches beneath

our boots as we wander.

Each holiday wreath

Says, "Welcome! Come visit

and share our GOOD CHEER!"

A walk in the winter

When CHRISTMAS is here.

Wheaton Malahy

Joy is not in things; it is in US.

Benjamin Franklin

A joy that's shared is a JOY made double.

English Proverb

WARM

holiday MEMORIES

make the very best

GIFTS of all —

though they're very hard to wrap!

Montague Cervantes

ARMS *are full* of bundles

Hearts with love o'erflow —

The real old Christmas SPIRIT

Sets our hearts **aglow.**

From an old Christmas postcard

Christmas Countdown

Eight tiny reindeer flying through the sky,
Seven falling snowflakes wave as they pass by. . .
Six singing children squeal with cheer and GLEE. . . .
Five pretty presents wait beneath the tree.
Four little KISSES under mistletoe,
Three pumpkin pies now cooling in a row,
Two cups of cocoa warm us in the night —
One tree BEJEWELED makes the season bright!

Lori Eberhardy

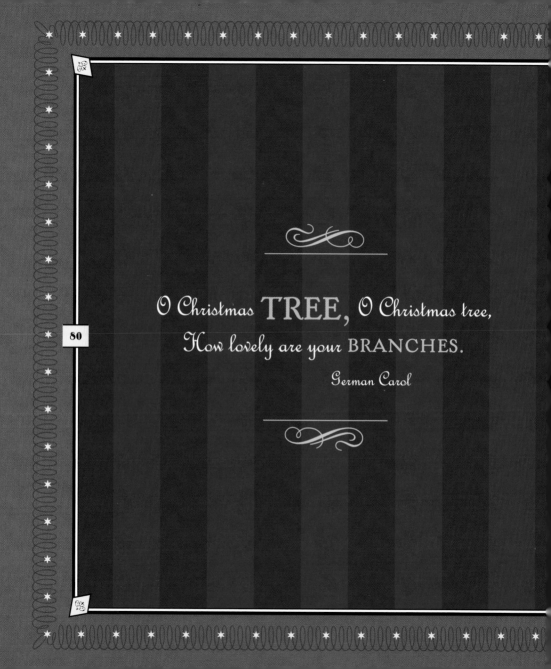

O Christmas TREE, O Christmas tree,
How lovely are your BRANCHES.

German Carol

Mistletoe

Just a SPRIGHTLY sprig of holly

Can help make the season jolly,

Christmas candles set the HOLIDAYS aglow. . .

But for those who need a reason

To put LOVE into the season,

Nothing does the trick as well as mistletoe!

Jan Miller Girando

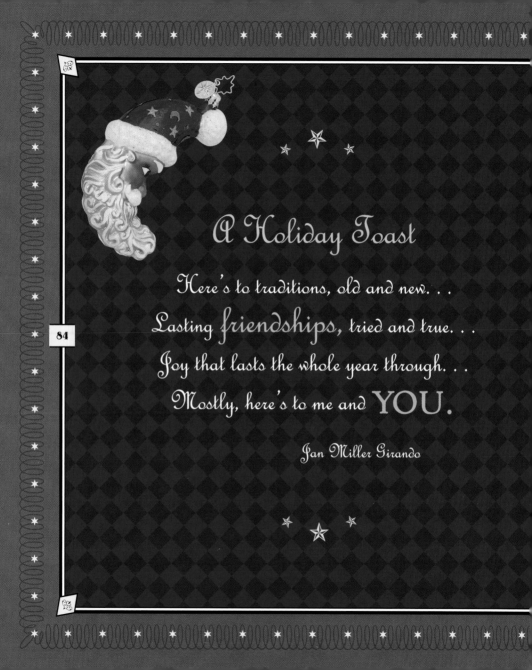

A Holiday Toast

Here's to traditions, old and new. . .

Lasting *friendships*, tried and true. . .

Joy that lasts the whole year through. . .

Mostly, here's to me and YOU.

Jan Miller Girando

84

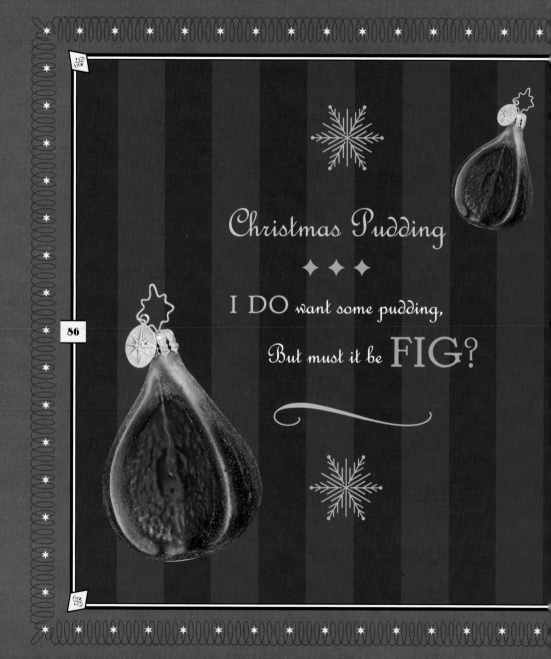

Christmas Pudding

◆ ◆ ◆

I DO want some pudding,

But must it be FIG?

If it was chocolate,

I'd eat like a PIG!

Charlie Colborne

Christmas Morning

The snowy hillsides glisten in the sunrise —
Jack Frost has painted fields a pearly white.
In every home, a Christmas tree is GLOWING
As children open presents with delight.

The table's set with all the family's finest,
And ready for the feast that's yet to be . . .
Another Christmas morning is becoming
Another CHERISHED Christmas memory.

Carroll Lincoln

Heap on more wood! — The WIND is chill;
But let it whistle as it will,
We'll keep our Christmas MERRY still.

Sir Walter Scott

·⌃⌃⌃⌃⌃⌃⌃·

I will honor Christmas in my heart,
and try to KEEP it all the year.

Charles Dickens
A Christmas Carol

Hearts aglow at Christmas

HEARTS aglow at Christmastime,
Spirits warm in wintry clime,
The world enraptured, lifts its voice —
Heav'n and earth with CHEER rejoice.

Montague Cervantes

Quiet Christmas Moments

Quiet Christmas moments
for GAZING at the tree.
Decorations lead us
to cherished reverie.

In such a busy SEASON,
it's nice to reminisce,
Enjoying Christmas memories
that came from times like this.

Charlie Colborne

96